mabel
murple

Sheree F

and

Maryann K

Doubleday Canad

Canadian Cataloguing in Publication Data

Fitch, Sheree
    Mabel Murple

Hardcover ISBN 0-385-25480-6; Paperback ISBN 0-385-25634-5

1. Children's poetry, Canadian (English).*
I. Kovalski, Maryann. II. Title.

PS8561.I83M3 1995 jC811'.54 C95-930187-9
PZ8.3.F57MA 1995

Design by Sharon Foster
Printed and bound in Canada by Printcrafters Inc.

Published by Doubleday Canada Limited,
105 Bond Street, Toronto, Ontario, M5B 1Y3

PRI 10 9 8 7 6 5 4 3

What if ...

There was a purple planet
With purple people on it

Would those purple people play
Whatever purple way they wanted?

And what if...

EVERYTHING was purple
I mean a WHOLE PURPLE WORLD
And there was someone just like me
I mean a purple sort of girl

There was a purple girl
How purple could she be?
Would she get in purple trouble?
(She would, if she were me!)

This purple girl should have a name
What name could rhyme with purple?
I must dream up a proper name . . .

I'VE GOT IT!

Now that I have named her
I will dream of what she's like . . .
Would Mabel Murple ride upon
Her purple motorbike?

Mabel Murple motored merrily
Through muddy purple puddles
She sang: "I'm a purple person!

She wore a purple helmet
And purple leather gloves
She's the purple motorbiker
Whom everybody loves!

"I'll roarrrrr away my troubles!"

(What is that purple blur?
Mabel Murple — yes! It's her!)

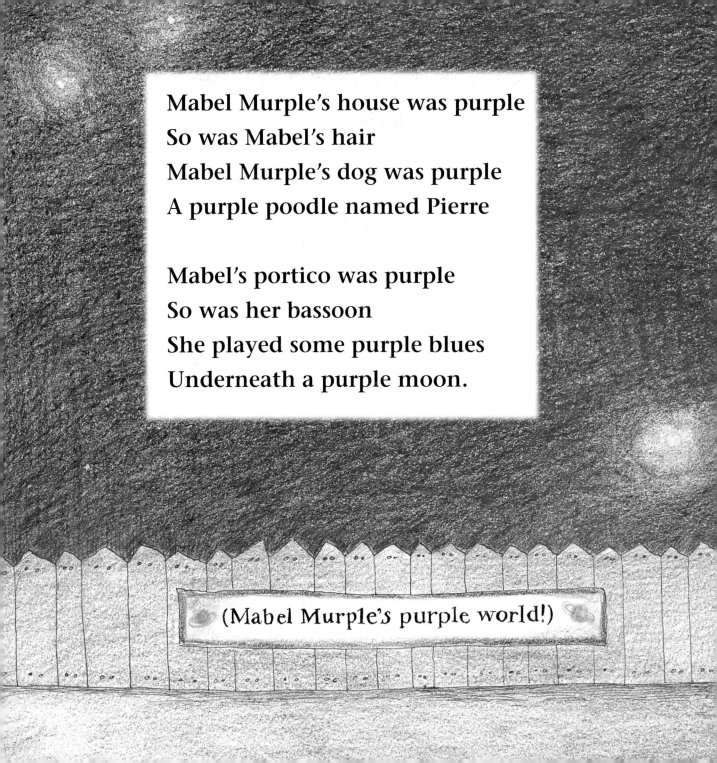

Mabel Murple's house was purple
So was Mabel's hair
Mabel Murple's dog was purple
A purple poodle named Pierre

Mabel's portico was purple
So was her bassoon
She played some purple blues
Underneath a purple moon.

(Mabel Murple's purple world!)

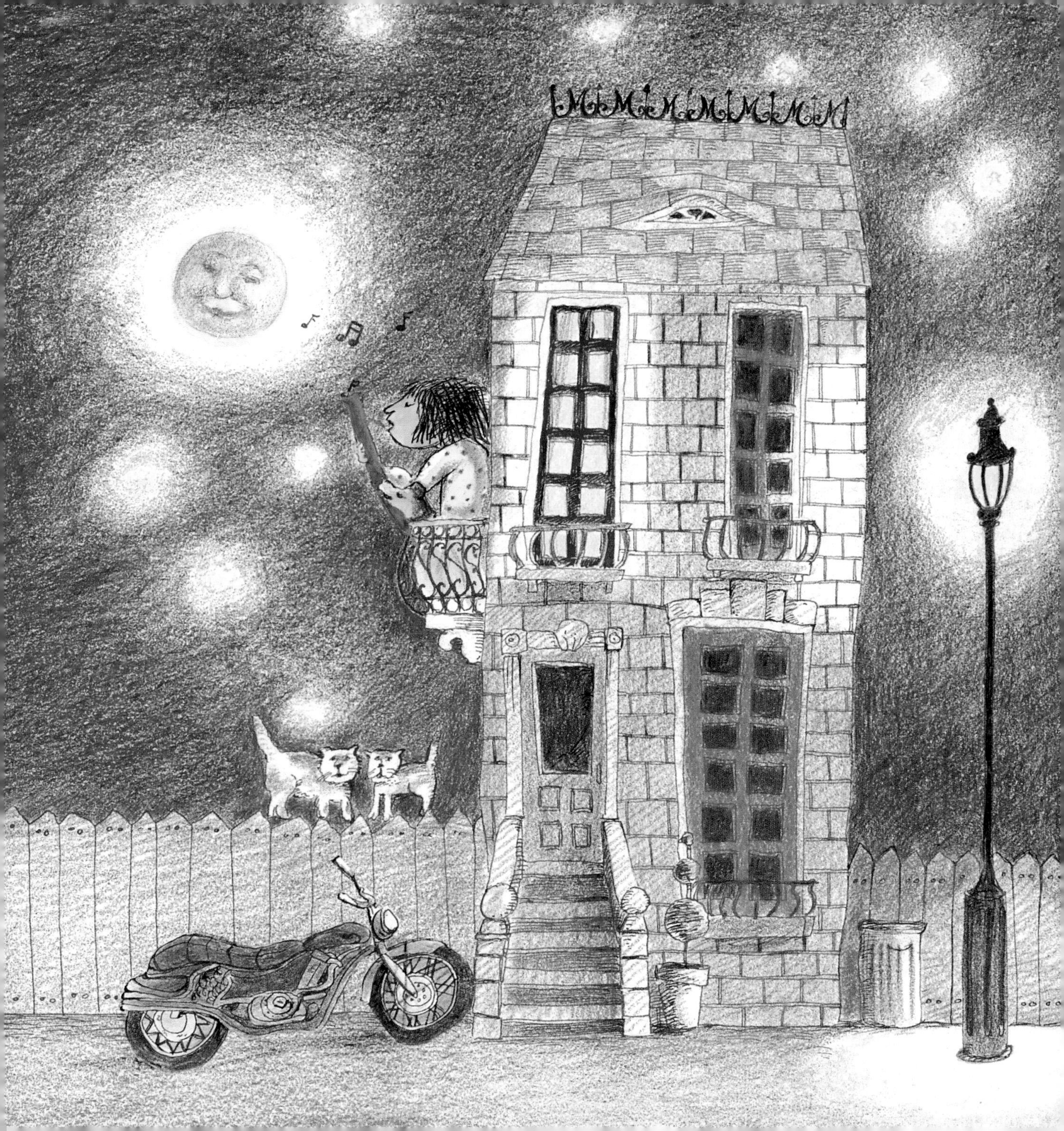

Mabel Murple had a skateboard
She skittered down the street
She wore a pair of purple sneakers
Upon her purple feet

She bumpled to a purple store
Then she slurpled purple juice

People shouted, "Skateboard Scallywag!
Mabel Murple's on the loose!"

(And they skedaddled!)

Mabel Murple ordered breakfast
She had purple eggs on toast
And when she ordered dinner
She had purple short rib roast

Mabel Murple cooked a supper
Murple's super duper purple stew
It was served with purple ketchup
And Mabel's maple syrple, too!

(Mabel Murple's purple syrple!)

Mabel Murple's skis were purple

She skied on purple snow

She wore a pair of purple goggles

And shouted, "Yee-haw, here I go!"

Mabel jumpled purple moguls

She slid on purple ice

Then she asked a ski instructor

For professional advice

(He said, "Slow down!")

Mabel Murple's room was purple
So was Mabel's bed
She slept with purple pillows
Beneath her purple head

She wore purple-dot pyjamas
And polka-purple socks
She had a purple teddy bear
Named Snickerknickerbox!

(And he **SNORED!**)

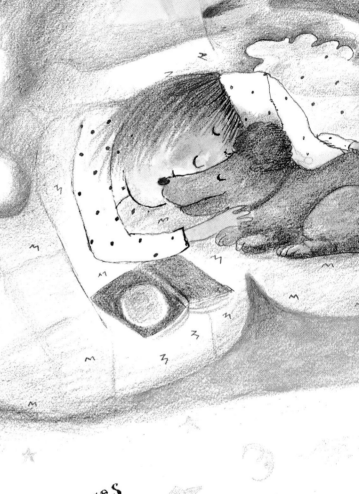

Even Mabel Murple
Has to close her eyes
I wonder if she dreams
Of distant purple skies?

Perhaps she dreams of places
She has never been
Of a world with multicolours
That she has never seen

Or perhaps when Mabel Murple dreams

She dreams of...

Gertrude Green!

Gertrude Green's house was green
So was Gertrude's hair
Gertrude Green's cat was green
So was her ... underwar

Imagine for a minute another kind of world

... A purple world, with purple people and places. In *Mabel Murple* young girl dreams of just that–with some wonderfully wacky resu

Sheree Fitch is a writer, poet, performer and creator of many stories for children and adults, including *Sleeping Dragons All Around*, *Toes in my Nose*, *Merry-Go-Day* and *I Am Small*. In 1993 she won the Mr. Christie Book Award for *There Were Monkeys in My Kitchen!* She lives in Halifax, Nova Scotia.

Maryann Kovalski is the author and illustrator of more than twenty books for children, including *The Wheels on the Bus*, *Take Me Out to the Ball Game*, *The Big Storm*, *The Cake That Mack Ate*, *Pizza for Breakfast* and *Doctor Knickerbocker*. She lives in Toronto, Ontario.

How Mabel Came to Be

I met Mabel Murple seventeen years ago when she presented herself in purple living colour in my notebook of poems and doodles and dreams and thoughts. Other people met her when she ended up in *Toes in my Nose*. The first Mabel poem went like this:

> Mabel Murple's house was purple
> So was Mabel's hair
> Mabel Murple's cat was purple
> Purple everywhere
> Mabel Murple's house was purple
> So were Mabel's ears
> And when Mabel Murple cried
> She cried terrible purple tears

Since then I have had so much fun performing this and so many people have written in response to Mabel that she and I have decided to tell more of her tongue-twisty tales. I hope you enjoy them. I hope they make you want to write your own.

Yours in purple propinquity,

Doubleday Canada Limited

Design by Sharon Foster
Printed and bound in Canada

ISBN 0-385-25634-5

9 780385 256346

50495

US$4.